AF481430

Short Stories

Calanthe Mavis

Published by Ray Young, 2021.

While every precaution has been taken in the preparation of this book, the publisher assumes no responsibility for errors or omissions, or for damages resulting from the use of the information contained herein.

SHORT STORIES

First edition. March 24, 2021.

Copyright © 2021 Calanthe Mavis.

ISBN: 979-8201165468

Written by Calanthe Mavis.

Table of Contents

BEFORE YOU BEGIN READING

Hello, dear friends! Welcome to my newest self-published book! Before you begin reading, there are a few things you should know:

As I am writing this note, I am under a 14-day quarantine and so are many other people. Yes, that's right. Right now, as I am writing this note to you, it's March 2020 and our biggest enemy appears to be COVID-19. As I am writing this, many foreign students cannot be with their families right now. Every day the police checks whether or not I am at home, because I am under a quarantine and so is everyone who has come back home from a risky country (I came home from France).

I wish everyone who is reading this little book of mine to stay strong. Together, we can overcome this. God gives us obstacles only if he knows we can overcome them!

You can follow me on my social media accounts if you want to connect with me.

WATTPAD: @keepfaithbaby and @calanthemavis
YOUTUBE: @keepfaithbaby
PINTEREST: @EtherealWriter
Thank you for purchasing the book and I hope you enjoy it! Stay safe!
#StayInside
XOXO,
Calanthe Mavis

1

"Sorry" never fixes a broken heart.

2

She just grew up differently.

3

Don't be afraid to explore even the tiniest streets - you never know what's around the corner.

4

He loved her, alas she loathed him with a burning passion.

5

You're jealous of them but you know nothing about them.

6

Who knows - they might be just like you?

7

I know it's hard, but suicide is never the option.

8

Band-aids and long sleeves have never fixed a scar.

9

Knives can be so alluring.

10

One cigarette is enough to start it all.

11

She wrote poems - now she's writing on the wall.

12

He wrote songs, but none of them were for you.

13

Always think before you speak.

14

Only the strongest will get out of this fight.

15

Never be fooled by one's appearance.

16

Secrets can make or break a relationship.

17

I'm more than you think I am.

18

A person is more than their hair, their skin colour, their clothes, their body.

19

I never learned what true love is.

20

Strength comes from experience, so the more you've overcome, the stronger you become.

21

He wishes there was something in his life to make him smile - just anything.

22

She came into his life just when he needed somebody.

23

He wanted her, but she wanted no one.

24

How do you go on when you've lost everything?

25

Take a deep breath - it always helps.

26

It's okay if you're not quite where you want to be in life - just keep on working hard and you'll get there, I promise.

27

It's a nightmare when food turns into the only comfort.

28

It's too late - you've done enough.

29

He said too much... and now he regrets it.

30

A word can silence one forever.
31

31

It always rains when someone cries for help - it's a sign to be followed.

32

The Internet is ugly.

33

Everyday she grows, but not the way she wants to.

34

He wanted someone so badly... but he could never have him, he was taken by another.

35

And she left him in the dust - just like that... pretending he never existed, pretending all they had was a spect of her imagination.

36

And she died miserably ever after...

37

School ended, but life never did.
38

38

Go back in real life, kid - fairytales aren't for everybody.

39

Do you ever regretting taking the first sip?

40

Famous people are the worst - they try to pretend everything is okay, even when it clearly isn't and that makes you feel horrible for yourself, it makes you feel insecure that you're not like them, that if you're not like them, Society won't approve of you.

41

I wish I stayed the same.

42

Ghosts aren't trying to be scary on purpose - they're only trying to convey messages for their loved ones from the afterlife.

43

Dad... you didn't have to hit Mom.

44

No, don't inject this - you will make the biggest mistake of your life!

45

Why do you hate me so much?

46

I'll never forget the blood on my hands.

47

She had gone too far, but so had he.

48

Did it hurt... did it hurt when you fell from heaven?

49

One photo can say it all.

50

I'm with you... never forget that... ever.

51

I don't want this to end... like... ever.

52

Sadly, everything comes to an end.

53

And the end is coming soon.

54

And this is the end.

AFTER YOU FINISH READING

This book was written back in the summer of 2019. Originally, I published it on Sweek (that was the site where my ex-boyfriend published a story and encouraged me to try it out). Then, I decided to publish it on Wattpad as well, since I am mostly there.
These short stories are only a sentence long, but I hope they have been relatable and inspiriting for you.
Before you close this little book of mine, possibly forever, I would like to wish you a great day or evening or night... depending on your time zone!
See you in my next book!
Calanthe Mavis

www.ingramcontent.com/pod-product-compliance
Lightning Source LLC
Chambersburg PA
CBHW052129150726
48002CB00006B/2535